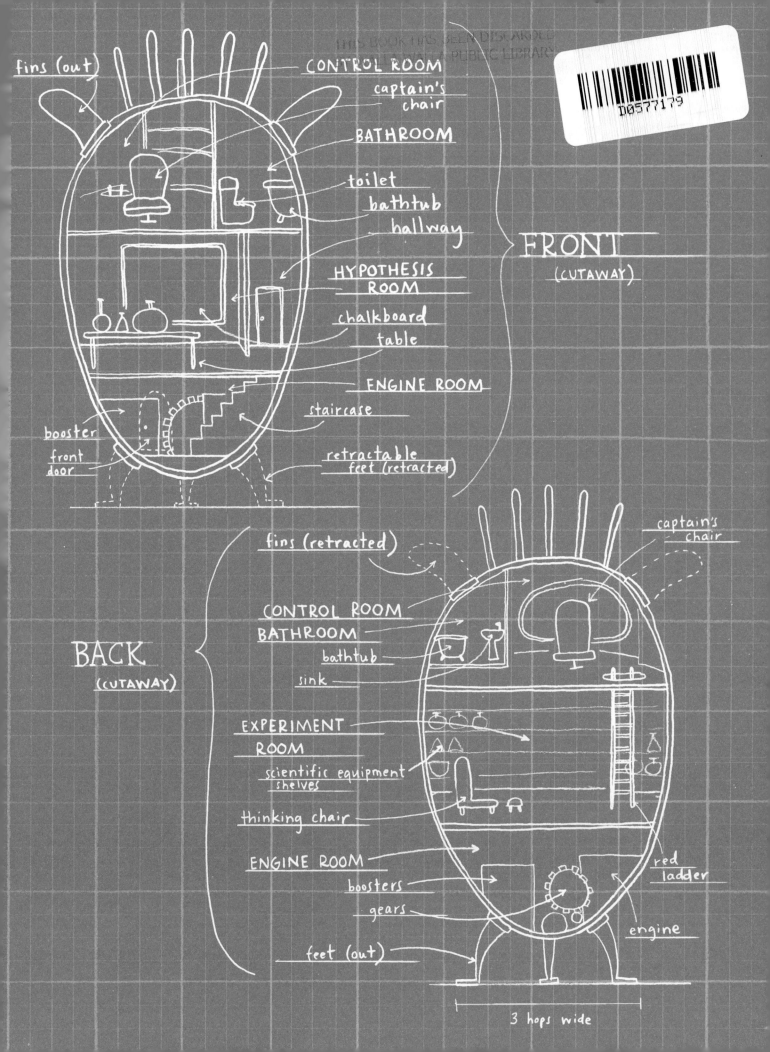

fins (out)

CONTROL ROOM
captain's chair

BATHROOM

toilet
bathtub
hallway

FRONT
(CUTAWAY)

HYPOTHESIS ROOM
chalkboard
table

ENGINE ROOM

staircase

booster
front door

retractable feet (retracted)

fins (retracted)

captain's chair

BACK
(CUTAWAY)

CONTROL ROOM
BATHROOM
bathtub
sink

EXPERIMENT ROOM

scientific equipment shelves

thinking chair

ENGINE ROOM
boosters
gears

red ladder

engine

feet (out)

3 hops wide

CHARLOTTE THE SCIENTIST IS SQUISHED

by **Camille Andros**

Illustrated by
Brianne Farley

CLARION BOOKS | Houghton Mifflin Harcourt
Boston   New York

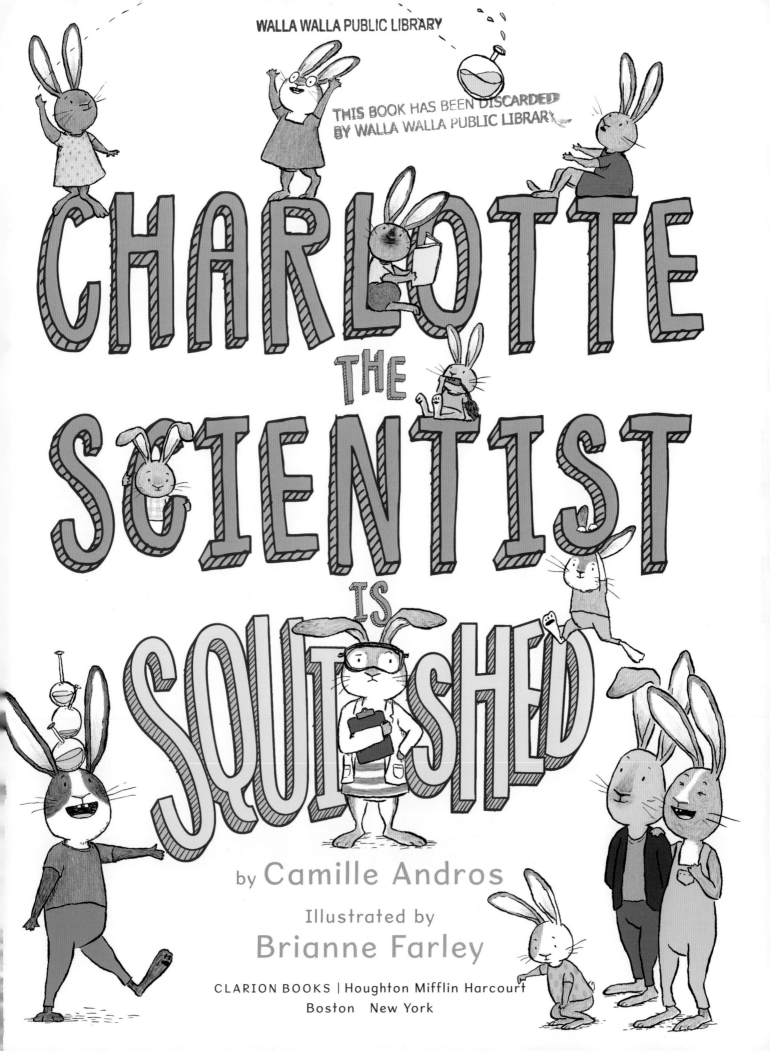

Charlotte was a serious scientist.

Protective glasses, a lab coat, and a magnifying glass were her essential scientific equipment. Plus a clipboard for important notes.

Charlotte solved problems by conducting experiments that followed the scientific method.

And Charlotte had a problem.

She was squished.

She was squished at the table.

She was squished in the tub.

And sometimes she was even squished on the toilet!

It had become impossible
to conduct her experiments.
Her test tubes were taken,
her beakers got broken, and her
specimens were spoiled.
Charlotte needed some space.
Time to use the scientific method!

STEP 1:
Ask a QUESTION.

STEP 2:
Form a HYPOTHESIS.

STEP 3:
Test the hypothesis—EXPERIMENT!

She tried an experiment to make everyone disappear . . .

. . . but it didn't work.

She tried another experiment to make herself disappear.

But that didn't work either.

If she was going to get some space . . .

. . . she would have to go there.

STEP 4:
Make and record OBSERVATIONS.

Charlotte was no longer squished at the table.

She was no longer squished in the tub.

And Charlotte could take as long as she wanted on the toilet.

Space was splendid!

STEP 5:
DRAW CONCLUSIONS.

She had all the room she needed
to conduct very important experiments
using her protective glasses, lab coat,
and magnifying glass.

Her test tubes were tidy, her beakers
looked brilliant, and her specimens
were sparkling.

Her hypothesis was correct! She
finally had room to be a scientist.

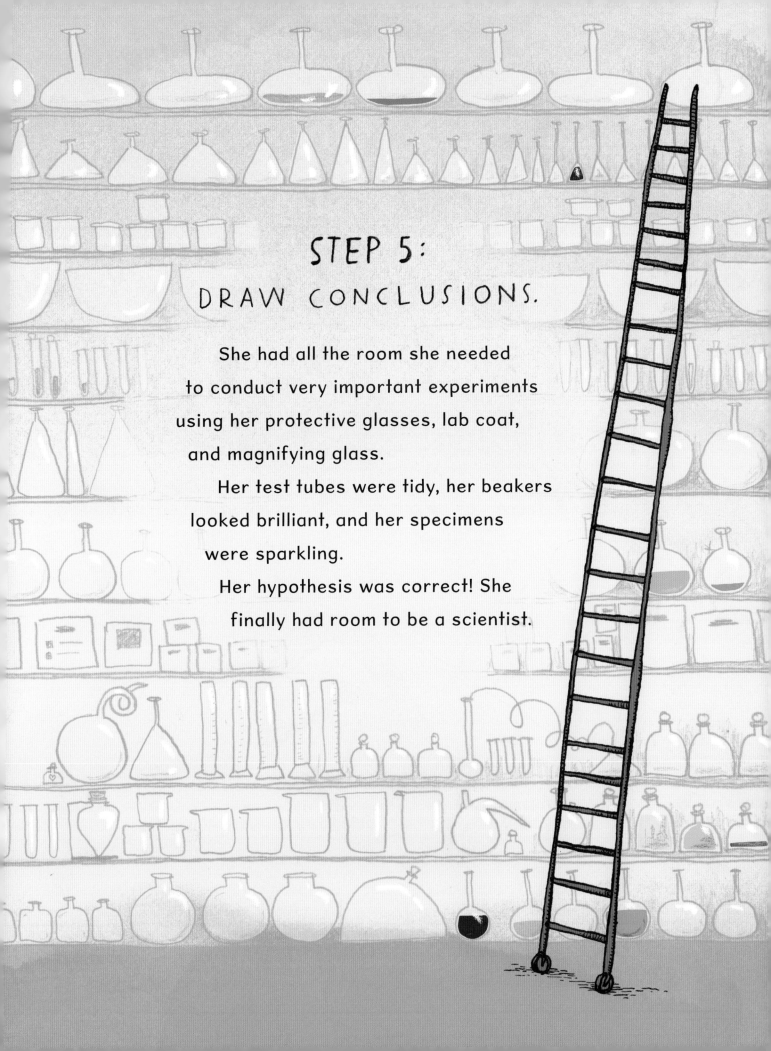

The only problem was . . .

there was no one to talk to at mealtime.

No one to blow bubbles with in the tub.

And what was Charlotte supposed to do when she ran out of toilet paper?

Space was lonely!

Time for more experiments!

Charlotte tried chocolate, but it was too tempting.
The balloons kept floating away.

And robot bunnies were poor conversationalists.
They got ruined in the bathtub and tangled in
the toilet paper.

BOOP

Charlotte missed her family.

She even . . . *missed* being squished.

So, she tried one last experiment . . .

And reached a new conclusion.

Charlotte didn't need outer space . . .

. . . she just needed her *own* space.

IN THE LAB WITH
CHARLOTTE

Being a scientist means asking questions and looking for answers. Scientists ask all kinds of questions. They ask to find out how something works, or how they can make something work better, or how they can help people. Some scientists study nature, like animals, insects, and plants. Others study stars and planets. Some find cures for diseases. Still others fly into outer space, or dig for dinosaur bones, or build robots and rockets. Every scientist starts by asking questions.

THE FIVE STEPS OF THE SCIENTIFIC METHOD

STEP #1: Ask a QUESTION.
What, when, who, which, why, where, or how?

Charlotte asked, "How can I get some space around here?"

STEP #2: Form a HYPOTHESIS.
A hypothesis is a best-guess answer to the question. Usually it includes the words "If" and "then."

Charlotte's first hypothesis was, "**If** I can get rid of my brothers and sisters, **then** I will have room to be a scientist."

What was Charlotte's second hypothesis?

STEP #3: Test the hypothesis—EXPERIMENT.
An experiment is a test to help find the answer to the question.

Charlotte tried an experiment to make herself disappear.

What other experiments did Charlotte do to help answer her question?

STEP #4: Make and record OBSERVATIONS.
Carefully watch and write down what happens during the experiment.

When Charlotte went to space, she noticed she had lots of room to be a scientist, but she was lonely.

What did Charlotte observe in her other experiments?

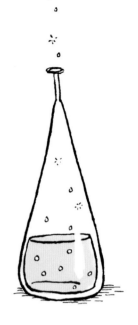

STEP #5: Form a CONCLUSION.
A conclusion is the information learned from the experiment.

What was Charlotte's big conclusion at the end of the story?

I want to know how YOU are being a scientist—at home, with your friends, or in your classroom. Follow the scientific method to answer a question, then write and tell me all about it.

CHARLOTTE THE SCIENTIST
c/o CLARION BOOKS/HMH
3 Park Avenue, 19th Floor,
New York, NY 10016

Or email me!
charlotte@charlottethescientist.com

To all young scientists,
especially my own.
—C. A.

To friends, family,
and alone time.
—B. F.

Clarion Books, 3 Park Avenue, 19th Floor, New York, New York 10016 • Text copyright © 2017 by Camille Andros • Illustrations copyright © 2017 by Brianne Farley All rights reserved. For information about permission to reproduce selections from this book, write to trade.permissions@hmhco.com or to Permissions, Houghton Mifflin Harcourt Publishing Company, 3 Park Avenue, 19th Floor, New York, New York 10016. • Clarion Books is an imprint of Houghton Mifflin Harcourt Publishing Company. • www.hmhco.com • The illustrations in this book were executed in charcoal, pencil, and ink on paper and colored digitally. • The text was set in Sweater School. • Design by Sharismar Rodriguez • Library of Congress Cataloging-in-Publication Data: Names: Andros, Camille, author. | Farley, Brianne, illustrator. • Title: Charlotte the scientist is squished / Camille Andros ; Brianne Farley. • Description: Boston ; New York : Clarion Books, Houghton Mifflin Harcourt, [2017] • Summary: "Charlotte, a serious scientist and a bunny, uses the scientific method to solve her problem: being squished by her many brothers and sisters"—Provided by publisher. • Identifiers: LCCN 2015045603 ISBN 9780544785830 (hardcover) • Subjects: | CYAC: Science—Methodology—Fiction. Science—Experiments—Fiction. Brothers and sisters—Fiction Family life—Fiction. | Rabbits—Fiction. • Classification: LCC PZ7.1.A565 Ch 2017DDC [E]—dc23 | LC record available at https://lccn.loc.gov/2015045603 Manufactured in China • SCP 10 9 8 7 6 5 4
4500713908

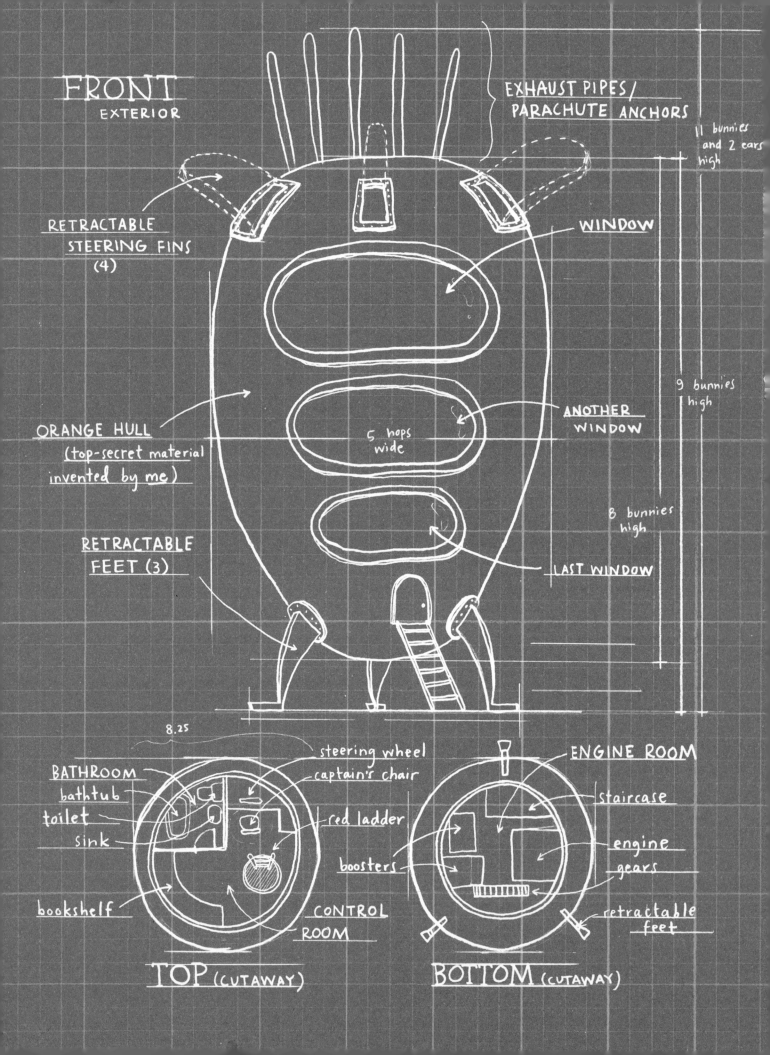